# Haffertee
# Goes Exploring

Haffertee  iamond made him for h...........g................(.........ond Yo), when her real pet hamster died.

In this book – the third in the series – Haffertee ventures further afield. Spotted Dog, Samson the tortoise and a black seagull called Fred make their first appearance. Haffertee learns about other people and has a narrow escape in the World Outside.

The charm of the stories lies in the funny, lovable character of Haffertee himself, and in the special place God has in the affections of Diamond Yo and her family.

The
Diamond
Family

Fran          Ma

Diamond Yo
with
Hafferkee and
Howl Owl

Pops

Mark

Chris.

# Haffertee Goes Exploring

# Haffertee Goes Exploring

**By Janet and John Perkins**
Illustrations by Gillian Gaze

A LION PAPERBACK

Copyright © 1977 Janet and John Perkins

Published by
**Lion Publishing plc**
Icknield Way, Tring, Herts, England
ISBN 0 85648 492 X
**Lion Publishing Corporation**
1705 Hubbard Avenue, Batavia, Illinois 60510, USA
ISBN 0 85648 492 X
**Albatross Books Pty Ltd**
PO Box 320, Sutherland, NSW 2232, Australia
ISBN 0 86760 374 7

First edition 1977
Second edition 1979
This edition 1982
Reprinted 1983, 1984, 1985, 1986

Cover picture and illustrations by Gillian Gaze
Copyright © 1977 Lion Publishing

Printed and bound in Great Britain by
Collins, Glasgow

# Contents

It all began when Yo's pet hamster died. To cheer her up, Ma Diamond made a ginger-and-white soft-toy hamster. The new Haffertee Hamster Diamond proved to be quite a character – inquisitive, funny and lovable. From his home in Yo's bedroom – shared with his friend Howl Owl and a strange collection of toys – he set out to explore Hillside House and meet the family: Ma and Pops Diamond and Yo's older brothers and sister, Chris, Fran and Mark. His adventures in the house and garden, and the World Outside are told in four books of stories: *Haffertee Hamster Diamond, Haffertee Hamster's New House, Haffertee Goes Exploring* and *Haffertee's First Christmas*.

# Spotted Dog

Haffertee was sitting in his favourite chair in his Very Own Box. He was really one of the family now. Yo was special, of course, but they were all his family: Ma and Pops Diamond, Fran and Mark and Chris. And he had made so many friends, too. Their pictures smiled at him from the wall. Haffertee was very happy.

But just now he felt like exploring. He poked his head round the door. There was Howl Owl sitting on his shelf.

'Howl,' said Haffertee, 'will you come with me? I'm going to explore the back garden.'

Howl stretched his wings a little and nodded. It was a side-to-side 'No' nod, not an up-and-down 'Yes' one. 'I'm sorry,' he said, 'but I can't. I promised Duckbill Balance I would call and see him today. Why not wait until tomorrow? I could come with you then.'

But Haffertee felt like exploring *now*, today, and he said so.

'Much better not,' said Howl. 'You are rather small, you know. And there's no telling what you might meet out there.'

'Oh, I can take care of myself,' said Haffertee carelessly.

Howl did not answer, but it was easy to see what he was thinking. 'All right,' he said at last. 'Go on your own if you must. But don't say I didn't warn you.' And with that he flew off.

'What a fuss about nothing!' Haffertee thought, and he set off at once for the back garden.

Hillside House, where Haffertee and the Diamond family lived, got its name from the hill on which it was built, and the back garden was very steep. To get to the wire fence, right at the top, Haffertee had to climb a lot of stone steps. That made him puff!

So, when he got to the raspberry canes, he decided to have a rest. It was a lovely day for resting and thinking.

Haffertee lay down on the warm ground. He was lying there peacefully, resting and thinking, when the spotted dog from up the road came into the garden.

He was a very large dog.

He was a very thin dog.

He was also a very hungry dog.

Haffertee watched him anxiously. 'I wonder if dogs eat hamsters?' he thought to himself.

He wasn't too sure of the answer, so he looked round for a place to hide, just in case. There was a rhubarb patch just below the place where he was resting.

'That's where I'll hide,' he decided quickly – and rustled in under the big leaves. He sat very still in the cool shade. He could hear the dog muzzling about. Suddenly there was a loud clatter. It sounded like the dustbin lid.

'Goodness me,' trembled Haffertee. 'He must be very hungry if he wants to eat the rubbish in the dustbin.'

Then he heard the dog's feet coming nearer and nearer, up the steps. 'Oh! I hope he doesn't come in here,' swallowed Haffertee.

The leaves above his head began to quiver. He could feel the dog's hot breath all round him. A big black-and-white spotted face peered down at him. Haffertee was just too scared to move.

Spotted Dog sniffed him closely up and down and round and round. Then, as suddenly as he had come, he was gone again. Haffertee *was* glad.

'I don't like spotted dogs,' he whispered to the rhubarb leaves. Then a little louder . . . 'I don't like spotted dogs!'

When he was quite sure that the dog had gone, Haffertee came out from under the leaves and began to sing loudly . . .

'I don't like spotted dogs.
I don't like spotted dogs.
Especially if they sniff you in the rhubarb.
No! I don't like spotted dogs!'

Then he scurried down the steps and back to Diamond Yo's room as fast as he could go.

Howl Owl was back from visiting his friend Duckbill Balance and he was talking to Yo about the journey. When Haffertee puffed his way into the room the two of them stopped talking and looked at him.

'Hello!' said Yo. 'What has made you so hot and bothered?'

'Oh, nothing much,' said Haffertee. 'Nothing that matters.'

'Something has frightened you,' said Howl slowly. 'Come on now Haffertee, tell us all about it.' At that, the words just came tumbling out, and the story was soon told.

'I was so frightened,' said Haffertee at last. 'So very frightened.'

'You needn't have been,' said Yo quietly. 'God was looking after you.'

'Oh,' said Haffertee. 'How can you be so sure?'

'Because I asked him to,' said Yo. 'And he is very reliable.'

Haffertee glanced quickly at Howl Owl. 'Next time I go exploring in the back garden, then, there will be three of us,' he said happily. 'You and me and God.'

# Haffertee Meets
# a Very Strange Creature

Howl Owl was up on the shelf above the door. He was fast asleep.

'Good morning, Howl,' said Haffertee. There was no reply. 'Good morning, Howl,' said Haffertee again.

Howl opened one eye, looked round to see who had made the noise, closed it and went back to sleep again.

'Good morning, Howl,' shouted Haffertee.

Both eyes opened this time and Howl found his voice. 'Good morning, Haffertee. Just let me have a stretch and a yawn and then I'll be down.'

A stretch and a yawn and Howl Owl fluttered down.

'There's something we must do today,' he said.

'Oh!' replied Haffertee. 'What's that?'

'We must go down to the garage to see Samson,' said Howl. 'He very much wants to meet you.'

Samson was Yo's tortoise. In winter he lived under an old mackintosh in an old bath in the garage. The summer was spent out of doors on the grass. Samson wasn't exactly quick, but was very old and wise. What he liked best was giving advice. He spent his spare time playing chess with Howl Owl.

The trouble with Samson was that he wandered. He soon grew tired of his own garden and when no one was looking he would wander off into someone else's. In case he got lost, Pops Diamond had painted a big '63' on his back, so that anyone who found him could bring him back to number 63 – Hillside House.

Howl and Haffertee made their way to the garage and opened the door. Inside, sure enough, was the old bath tub and the old mackintosh, and underneath was Samson.

All Haffertee could see was a tough-looking shell with the number '63' painted on it. He was very surprised. He had never seen anything like Samson before. The tortoise had no legs, and no head either.

'Where is his head?' asked Haffertee.

At the sound of his voice Samson's hard shell began to move slowly upwards. A leathery old face popped out at one end and four legs appeared, one at each corner.

'Goodness me,' said Haffertee. 'What a funny thing. How does he do that?'

Howl frowned at Haffertee and flapped his wing to his beak. 'Ssshhh!' he said. 'It's rude to talk like that.'

Samson began to move his head slowly up and down . . . up and down . . . sideways and wideways . . . sideways and narrow-ways . . . But still he did not speak.

'What an ugly face!' said Haffertee, taking no notice as Howl Owl shook his head at him. 'It's all shrivelled up.'

Samson just rolled his eyes.

'Gosh,' said Haffertee, still staring at Samson. 'You *are* old!'

Howl could stand it no longer. He jumped up and down on both feet, hopping mad. 'Samson,' he said hurriedly, before Haffertee could say any more. 'Meet my new friend Haffertee. Haffertee,' Howl continued, 'this is my old friend Samson.'

Samson stood completely still and said nothing.

Haffertee waited and then turned to Howl. 'Why doesn't he *say* something?' he asked.

'I will say something when I have something to say,' said the old tortoise in a slow, deliberate voice. 'When *I* talk I try to talk sense.' He moved closer to Haffertee. 'I am very pleased to meet you,' he said. 'Very pleased indeed. Any friend of Howl's is a friend of mine.'

For once, Haffertee had nothing to say. But he was bursting with questions. Before he could get the first one out, Howl Owl hurried him away.

'I think we had better leave Samson to get on with

his tea,' he said firmly. And he almost dragged Haffertee out of the garage and back to Diamond Yo's room.

'Haffertee!' he burst out, when they were safely out of hearing. 'Why ever did you say all those nasty things to Samson? You were very rude. I don't know what Samson will think. You have no manners at all!'

And before Haffertee could argue or ask questions or even get a word in edgeways, Howl huffed off to the shelf above the door, tucked his head under his wing and sat quite still. He obviously wasn't talking.

Haffertee had plenty of time to think about what Howl had said. Perhaps he *had* been rather rude. At bedtime Haffertee told Yo all that had happened.

'What did I say wrong?' he asked. 'Samson *is* old and skinny. And he does look ugly.'

'Even if he does, you needn't have said so,' answered Yo. 'It's not always kind to say the first thing that comes into your head, you know. It can hurt people's feelings. And anyway, looks aren't everything. Samson may look strange but he's really very nice. And he's a very good friend. You ask Howl Owl.'

Next morning Haffertee woke Howl Owl very

early, just to say sorry. Together they went to the garage.

Haffertee wanted to make up for being so rude. 'Samson,' he said, 'I've come to ask your advice . . .'

He couldn't have pleased the old tortoise more! Soon they were deep in conversation. Haffertee was quite sorry when the time came to say goodbye. He looked at Samson again, and somehow he didn't seem strange or ugly now. Samson and Haffertee were friends!

# Harvest Festival Time

It was Harvest Festival time and Yo was busy trying to explain to Haffertee exactly what that meant.

'This is the time of year,' she said, 'when we gather in all the fruit and vegetables before the winter comes and we thank God for giving us all we need.'

'Oh!' said Haffertee. 'That's very kind of him!'

Yo smiled. Haffertee was quite right, but he did have a funny way of saying things.

'At Harvest Festival time Mummy makes two special apple pies. One is called the Family Pie and the other is called the Church Pie. She is very good with pastry and likes making nice things for us to eat.'

Haffertee was just going to ask what a Church Pie was when Ma called to Yo from the kitchen.

'Will you go into the garden, Yo, and get me some apples, please?'

'All right,' called Yo. 'Just let me get my welling-ton boots on. Would you like to come with me, Haffertee? I'll need some help with "gathering in the harvest".'

'Yes, please,' said Haffertee. Gathering in the harvest sounded very grand. He didn't want to miss a bit of it.

Yo found a basket and went out into the garden. Haffertee trotted behind her. There were three apple trees at the top of the garden. Yo made for the one nearest the fence.

Haffertee was beginning to find walking rather difficult. His feet were picking up mud and mud and more mud. Before long he couldn't move his feet at all. He was stuck! There was nothing for it but to sit down and try to get the mud off. So that's what he did. He sat down and started scraping the mud off. And as he sat there, one of the ripe apples on the tree decided it was time to come down. It didn't look for an empty space. It just fell – plonk! – right on Haffertee's head.

'Ouch!' he shouted, as he rubbed his head. 'That was a heavy apple.'

Yo picked it up and put it in the basket. 'That's good,' she said. 'It isn't bruised at all!'

Haffertee gave her a funny look. He wanted to say, 'What about my head?' but he didn't. He didn't get the chance.

'Now then,' said Yo briskly. 'Up you go! Just shake a few of those apples down and I'll pick them up when they fall.'

Haffertee rubbed his head. He wasn't at all sure about climbing trees. He'd seen the Purrswell kittens playing in the branches and it looked easy enough. But he was a hamster and he wasn't so sure about hamsters climbing trees.

He didn't say anything, though. He just started to climb. It was easier than he'd thought and he was soon quite a long way off the ground. At least, that was how it seemed. And when he looked down, the ground was

a very long way off. He began to feel quite dizzy.

'Shake away, then, Haffertee,' called Yo. 'Shake away!'

Haffertee tried very hard to shake the branch he was holding on to, but it just wouldn't move. He pulled and pushed and shoved and tugged and . . . nothing! It just wouldn't budge.

'Come on, Haffertee,' shouted Yo. 'Get a move on or we'll never get the apples for Mummy's pies. Give it a good shake!'

Haffertee gritted his teeth and took a deep breath and heaved at the branch. It was then he felt his feet slipping. There was still a lot of mud on them and he just couldn't keep his balance. He fell backwards off the branch and head-over-heels-over-head-over-heels. Bump! That was the ground!

'Oh!' he said. 'OOOOOOOhhhh!'

Yo came over to look at him. 'Whatever are you doing coming down so soon?' she said. 'We haven't any apples yet. Here, you stay by the basket and I'll shake some of the branches.' And she started towards the middle of the tree.

Haffertee was only too glad to stay by the basket. Anything was better than climbing that tree again.

Yo caught hold of a branch and began to shake. She shook and shook and shook.

And the apples came down and down and down.

Right on top of Haffertee! Poor Haffertee! He just couldn't get out of the way in time. And before you could say, 'Basketful of apples', he was up to his ears in them.

'Why aren't you picking them up?' asked Yo, when she came over to get the basket. 'You *are* slow today.'

Haffertee just couldn't understand it. His feet were covered with mud. His head was covered with bumps, and Yo didn't seem to care at all. It wasn't his day. At last, the basket was full and they carried it into the kitchen.

Ma Diamond had already lined the pie dishes and was soon busy peeling and slicing the apples. She took one look at Haffertee's muddy feet and his bumpy head and frowned.

'Whatever happened to you, Haffertee?' she asked.

'Never mind,' she said, when he'd finished explaining. 'Just you wait until the pies are cooked. You'll think it was worth it then.'

So Haffertee watched and waited and waited and watched until at last Ma opened the oven door and pulled out the two lovely pies. They smelt delicious. And when Haffertee was given a taste, he was sure the bumps had been worth while.

Ma washed her hands, took off her apron, and they all sat down to tea. Then Ma closed her eyes and said, 'Thank you, God, for food to eat and for your promise that we shall always have a seed time and a harvest.'

'Yes!' said Haffertee, rubbing his bumps. Then he added quietly under his breath. 'But I do wish you'd make the harvest a bit easier to gather!'

# Fred,
# the Black Seagull

Yo's brother, Mark, had a seagull in his hands.

It didn't look like a seagull because it was black all over. Haffertee couldn't believe it was a bird at all. Yo didn't even think it was alive.

'Quick,' said Mark. 'Run and fetch some warm soapy water.'

Yo hurried off to the kitchen to do as Mark asked, while Haffertee stood there watching.

'Where did you find that?' he asked, when Mark had managed to put the messy bundle down on the ground by the flowerpots.

'I found him on the road by the front gate,' said Mark quickly. 'I was just going off on my bike when I saw this black bundle on the road in front of me. I wondered what it was, and when I got near it moved. I couldn't just leave it there on the road, so I picked it up and brought it home. Now look!' He beckoned Haffertee closer.

Haffertee had never been that close to a seagull before. He could just make out a head and a big grey beak. The beak was opening and closing feebly and a strange croaking noise was coming from the bird's throat. The eyes were only half open and they were

27

sad and hopeless. The feathers were all stuck together by a kind of black glue. The seagull's breathing was so weak he seemed hardly to move at all.

'Can't we do anything for him?' said Haffertee, sadly.

Yo suddenly appeared with a bowl of soapy water. She took a closer look at the bird.

'Ugghh!' she said. 'However did a seagull get into a mess like that?'

'It's oil,' said Mark. 'He must have got smothered with oil on one of the beaches and just struggled up on to the road. He certainly is in a mess. Come on now, Yo, you hold him while I try to clean him up.'

Haffertee stood back and watched as the two of them set to work. Gently they cleaned the oil from the bird's eyes, and sponged its head and wings. It was slow work but they made some progress. The water in the bowl grew blacker and the bird began to look whiter. The feathers separated a little and the wings began to pull apart. Even the throaty croaking noise grew less harsh.

At last, after what seemed a very long time, Mark put down the cloth he had been using and started to dry the bird with a towel.

'Right,' he said, when that was done. 'Now let's see if we can find something to put him in.'

Ma Diamond had been watching from the kitchen window. Now she opened the window and pushed out a cardboard box.

'Try that,' she said. 'If it fits, you can bring the box and the bird into the kitchen. Put him by the water heater, that should keep him warm. If he rests there for a day or two he'll probably get well again.'

The box did fit and the seagull slept all that day and through the night. At bedtime Yo asked God to take special care of Fred the Seagull.

Haffertee woke early next morning. But Yo was up already and so was Mark. That was really something – Mark up early on a Saturday morning!

Haffertee followed them quickly downstairs to the kitchen and straight to the box by the water heater. Fred the Seagull seemed quite bright and lively. He snapped his beak and gave them a hoarse, 'Good morning.'

'Oh, thank you, God,' said Yo, quietly. 'You've saved Fred's life.'

'Yes,' said Mark, and nodded.

In the days that followed, Haffertee, Mark and Yo spent a lot of time looking after Fred. He became very friendly and began to recognize them when they called.

'Krark, Mark,' he would say in his hoarse voice. 'Kroke Yo.' But he couldn't manage Haffertee's name!

Every day Fred grew stronger. Soon he was strutting about the kitchen on his own, and one day he got as far as the garden. Then the strutting turned to hopping and the hopping turned to flying – just a little way at first . . .

'It won't be long before he leaves us now,' said Mark, feeling rather sad.

'I shall miss him,' said Yo.

Haffertee said nothing.

But the day came when Fred hopped on to the wire fence and then flew into the apple tree. With one last look at the house, he flapped his wings, then soared up into the sky and away out of sight.

Fred the Seagull had gone. Mark and Yo kept watching but Fred was gone. Away out into the wild air and the free sky.

When he didn't come back, Haffertee was very disappointed. All that time Mark and Yo had spent cleaning Fred and taking care of him – when they might have been having fun.

'Why did you take all that trouble with Fred?' asked Haffertee one morning after breakfast.

Mark and Yo looked at each other. 'Why?' said Yo slowly. 'Well, why not?'

'Fred was there,' said Mark. 'And he needed help.

So we gave him some. Being kind to one of God's birds is like being kind to God himself.'

'Why?' asked Haffertee, quickly. 'Is God a seagull?'

Yo nearly fell off the seat. Mark grinned. And Pops Diamond laughed out loud.

'Is God a seagull?' he spluttered. 'You do get some strange ideas, Haffertee. God made the seagulls, so when one of them is hurt, God is sad. If you and I help a seagull then we make God happy again.'

'Can you find me a dirty seagull?' Haffertee asked suddenly. 'I think I would like to make God happy.'

'Keep looking around,' said Mark slowly. 'You'll find lots of ways to do that if you keep your eyes open.'

# Haffertee Breaks a Bracelet

Diamond Yo was very excited. The postman had just brought her a small parcel. She knew who had sent it but she didn't know what was in it. She pulled impatiently at the paper.

At last the parcel was open and Yo could see inside. There in a little box, on a bed of cotton wool, lay a lovely silver bracelet.

Yo gasped in surprise and delight. Very, very carefully she lifted it out of the box and slid it over her hand and on to her wrist. It was beautiful. Howl Owl and Haffertee thought it was beautiful too.

'Can I hold it?' Haffertee asked.

'Yes,' said Yo. 'But be very careful with it.'

Haffertee took it gently from her and held it in his hands. He was being very careful the bracelet didn't fall. So careful, he didn't notice how very close he was to the edge of the desk. He took a step back.

And before you could say, 'Ears and whiskers', Haffertee was gone. It was a long way down to the floor and half way down a hook stuck out from the side of the desk. Yo sometimes hung her scissors on it. The scissors weren't there today – Haffertee and the bracelet were, just for a minute. The bracelet caught

on the hook. Then it bent and snapped under
Haffertee's weight. Haffertee landed bump on the
floor, with the bracelet round his head.

Poor Haffertee. He felt awful.

Poor Yo. She felt dreadful.

Poor Howl. He felt so sorry for them both.

33

They stood for a long time looking at the broken bracelet.

Yo was the first to move. She picked the bracelet up and looked at it carefully. 'We can straighten it out, it's only the clip that's broken,' she said, at last. 'Never mind. It wasn't your fault, Haffertee. It was an accident.'

Yo was being very kind. Her beautiful new bracelet was spoilt, but she didn't tell Haffertee he should have looked where he was going.

'Thank you,' he said in a small voice, very upset.

'I'll ask Pops to take the bracelet to the jewellers tomorrow,' said Yo bravely. 'Perhaps they'll be able to mend it for me and I shall have it back again quite soon.'

Haffertee nodded and limped out of the room. He didn't see Yo's tears as soon as he had left.

The Purrswell kittens, Dominic, Tina and Smudge were playing Hide-and-Seek on the stairs. Haffertee was so wrapped up in his troubles he didn't even see them.

He stepped straight on to a furry back, toppled wildly, and shot off down the stairs in a mad succession of somersaults. Upple and topple and tipple and bobble. Over and over and bounce and bounce – to the bottom of the stairs in record time.

It was just too much. He picked himself up and shouted at the kittens.

'Don't you know it's dangerous playing Hide-and-Seek on the stairs? Haven't you anything better to do?' Haffertee was very cross indeed. The fur on the back of his neck stood up angrily.

The three kittens were quite taken aback. They crouched unhappily in a corner. They had never been scolded like that before. And Haffertee went on scolding and shouting.

The noise brought Howl and Yo downstairs to see what had happened. Yo had stopped crying, but the broken bracelet was still in her hand.

Haffertee stopped shouting when he saw them and began to feel a bit ashamed. Yo had been so kind about the bracelet. She hadn't shouted at him and been cross.

Haffertee caught his breath. 'I'm sorry, kittens,' he said softly. 'I shouldn't have been so cross. I should have looked where I was going.' The three Purrswell kittens began to purr again, and shot out into the kitchen.

Yo gave Haffertee a special hug and poggled his ears. Howl Owl put a friendly wing around him. There was no need to say anything. It had been a day of lessons.

It was Friday when the bracelet came back, mended and looking almost like new. Diamond Yo was so pleased. Haffertee didn't ask to hold it this time.

'You put it on, Yo,' he said instead, 'so that we can all see it.'

# The Box of
# Happy People

It was the very first day of the Half-Term Holiday and it was raining hard.

Diamond Yo was very disappointed. She'd been looking forward to exploring the beach with her friends. Howl Owl had planned a visit to Hunter's Lodge but he didn't want to get his wings wet. Haffertee had hoped to do some sunbathing in the garden near the raspberries.

Now Yo had gone shopping with Ma Diamond, and Haffertee and Howl Owl were left on their own, feeling very bored.

It was going to be one of those days! Haffertee could feel it in his fur; Howl could feel it in his feathers.

They just didn't know what to do, and they couldn't agree.

Soon they began to argue and shout. They had almost come to blows when Howl had his brainwave.

'Let's find Rabbearmonklio,' he said. (Rabbearmonklio lived in the Toy Cupboard. He had a rabbit's ears, a bear's body, the merry face of a monkey and a lion's long tail. Everyone loved him.) 'He's full of good ideas. He's sure to think of something we can do.'

Together, Haffertee and Howl went over to the Toy

Cupboard and knocked on the door.

'Come in,' said a soft voice. And in they went.

Rabbearmonklio was sitting on a large cushion, reading. He was a great reader.

'How can I help you?' he said, putting down his book.

Howl looked at Haffertee.

Haffertee looked at Howl.

Then they both began to explain together.

'Just one at a time please,' said Rabbearmonklio. 'Howl, you tell me what I can do for you.'

Howl took a deep breath. He explained about the wet day, and being bored. 'We can't think of anything to do,' he said. 'And we're feeling very cross.'

Rabbearmonklio looked at them both. 'I think I know how you feel,' he said. 'Yo felt just the same a little while ago and Pops got her making some Happy People.'

'Some Happy People?' said Howl and Haffertee together, in surprise.

'Yes,' said Rabbearmonklio. 'Some Happy People. Would you like to see them? Yo made them a few weeks ago on a rainy afternoon. She made a special box for them, too. They live here with us in the Toy Cupboard.'

Haffertee and Howl were very excited. This sounded interesting. A box of Happy People!

Rabbearmonklio called to someone at the back of the cupboard. A little monkey with a red jacket came towards them. He took out a mouth organ and started to play a very jiggy tune.

Haffertee recognized him at once. He had played for them all on the night of the Toy Cupboard Party.*

Rabbearmonklio went over to a large cardboard box in the corner of the Toy Cupboard and opened a door.

'Will you come and sing for us today?' he called.

Haffertee and Howl waited.

They weren't quite sure what was going to happen. Rabbearmonklio stepped back.

Then . . . one by one, out of the box came the strangest little creatures Haffertee and Howl had ever seen. They had yoghurt-carton bodies and egg-box heads. Their white cardboard hands and feet were enormous. And their clothes were the prettiest you have ever seen, all colours and shades and

*You can read this story in *Haffertee Hamster Diamond*.

sparkles. They had large pink ears, big wide smiles
and eyes like stars. They were all clapping their hands
and tapping their feet merrily in time with the music.
It was a wonderfully cheering sight and a wonderfully
cheering sound!

'These are the Happy People,' said Rabbearmonklio, proudly. 'They sing to cheer us up.'

Haffertee and Howl stood quite still and watched.

The Happy People clapped and clapped. They
sang and sang and they smiled and smiled. And then,
right in the middle of the fun, a great big golden sun
rolled out of the box, scattering light and shining
brightly. He made the dresses and skirts sparkle even
more. The smiles grew wider. Soon the whole place
was full of happy clapping people.

At the sight of those Happy People Haffertee and
Howl felt all cheered up inside. They forgot the rain.
They forgot being cross and bored. They began to
smile, and clap and sing. Soon they were laughing
and singing together!

40

Just then Yo put her head round the door. 'Oh!' she said. 'I see you've found my Happy People.'

Haffertee and Howl stopped whirling round. 'Yes!' they puffed together. 'Yes we have!'

Yo smiled. 'I made them when I was feeling down-in-the-dumps, to cheer myself up,' she said. 'And I made the sun to remind me that it doesn't always rain.'

But Howl and Haffertee weren't listening. They'd forgotten the rain long ago.

They were swinging and clapping and laughing with all those Happy People.

# Yo's Special Gang

Howl Owl was going somewhere special. He had polished his beak and smoothed his feathers. He looked very smart indeed.

'My word!' said Haffertee, when Howl came down from his shelf. 'You do look smart!'

'Thank you,' said Howl. 'I'm going to our Annual Dinner.'

'Annual Dinner?' said Haffertee. 'Whatever's that?'

'Weller . . .' said Howl, slowly. He was trying to think. 'Weller . . . It's a very special meeting. We have it once a year. We meet our friends and we have a feast of our favourite things and we share all the news. It's most enjoyable.'

'Is it an Owl Gang?' asked Haffertee.

Howl smiled. 'Yes,' he said. 'I suppose you could call it that. Just a lot of friendly owls having an evening out.'

'Oh well!' said Haffertee, with a sigh. 'I don't suppose they would let a hamster in, would they?'

'I'm afraid not,' said Howl, feeling just a little bit sorry for Haffertee. 'It is a very special gang, you see. You can only belong if you're an owl!'

'Oh well!' said Haffertee again. 'In that case I'll have to find a Hamster Gang and see if I can join that! Have a nice time, Howl.'

With that, Haffertee sat down on the bed and started to look through the pages of a colouring book which Yo had given him. He picked up a pencil and started to colour in a picture of a large meal.

Howl watched for a moment, then flew off downstairs and out of the kitchen to his very special Owl meeting.

Haffertee carried on quietly colouring. He heard the back door slam. And before he could say, 'Hello, Yo!' – which was what he wanted to say – the room was full of Yo's friends. There were so many of them, Haffertee was almost squashed. He slipped quickly under the bed, out of the way. No one seemed to notice him at all. Whatever was going on?

At first he could only make out a babble of voices. Odd words came floating down to him under the bed but nothing that seemed to make sense. Then he heard someone strumming away on a guitar. After a moment or so he heard Yo singing a song Chris Diamond had written.

Haffertee listened carefully. He heard Yo sing the first verse and then start on the chorus. Haffertee

knew it so well he just had to join in. At first he sang
very quietly, but after a little while he was singing
away at the top of his voice.

Suddenly he saw a row of heads. They were all
upside down, hanging from the side of the bed!

Yo's friends had found him. His singing had given
him away!

'Come on out of there, Haffertee,' said Yo, rather
firmly. 'What are you doing under the bed?'

'I was just listening to you singing,' said Haffertee,

quickly. 'I did try to get out when everyone came in but I couldn't, so I hid under here.'

Yo smiled. She knew that all her friends arriving in such a rush must have frightened Haffertee, so she picked him up gently and introduced him.

'Now then, Haffertee,' said Yo. 'Off you go, and let us get on with our practice. We have to get this song right. We're singing it at church on Sunday morning.'

Haffertee waved goodbye to his new friends and went straight down to the kitchen where he found Ma Diamond doing some mending.

'Hello, Haffertee,' she said, as he came in. 'Where have you been?'

Haffertee explained. 'What's going on upstairs?' he asked. 'Is it a special meeting or something, like Howl Owl's?'

'Not quite,' said Ma, trying to thread some more black cotton through the eye of the needle. 'Yo just invited some of her friends in from church. They're practicing a special song for Sunday.'

'Is it a kind of gang, then?' asked Haffertee.

'You could call it that,' said Ma. 'Yo's Special Gang.'

Haffertee thought about that for a moment.

'Could I join?' he asked, excitedly.

'I don't know,' said Ma. 'You had better ask Yo.'

So Haffertee did. When all the singing was over and Yo's friends had gone home, he asked Yo if he could join her Special Gang.

'Certainly,' said Yo. 'But you will have to pass a test first.'

'A test?' said Haffertee in surprise. 'What sort of test?'

'Well, our Gang is for singing,' said Yo. 'So you must show me you really can sing.'

Haffertee thought he was quite a good singer. 'Right,' he said. 'When do I start?'

'Here and now,' said Yo. 'Off you go.'

And Haffertee began to sing. He sang one of the happiest songs Yo had ever heard, and he sang it beautifully.

'If you can sing like that,' said Yo, 'you are *very* welcome to join our gang.'

And that was how Haffertee became a member of Diamond Yo's Special Gang. Every Sunday morning he goes to church with them to help them sing.

He loves it.

So now Howl Owl is not the only one who goes 'Somewhere Special'!

# Haffertee and the World Outside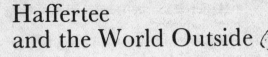

Haffertee and Howl Owl were sitting quietly on the window-sill in the front room watching the clouds go by. Someone was singing loudly in the garage. Haffertee waited for a gap in the singing and then said quickly, 'What's going on in the garage, Howl?'

Howl Owl rolled his eyes and shrugged his wings. 'I don't know,' he said, 'but we can soon find out. Let's go down and see.'

As they peered round the garage door they saw Chris Diamond working. He was polishing hard. This way and that way and the other way, all along the side of a little grey car. He was singing such a merry song.

'Hello!' said Haffertee, in between verses of the song. 'You do sound happy!'

'Why not?' said Chris, with a smile. 'I'm going to College on Saturday and I've just managed to save up enough money to buy this car to take me there.'

'Going to College!' said Haffertee in surprise. 'What's that? And why do you want to go there?'

'Good question,' said Chris. 'A very good question. Now let me try to give you a very good answer.' He stopped polishing the side of the car and put down the cloth. 'College is for studying things,' he said helpfully. 'I want to know how to be a lawyer.' Then he said, 'And I want to see a bit of the world outside.'

Haffertee wanted to ask what a lawyer was, but the last bit sounded more exciting. So he said, 'Will you take us for a ride in your car to the World Outside?'

'Certainly,' said Chris. 'Just let me finish polishing this side and then we'll go down to the village to get some stamps.'

Haffertee and Howl waited patiently on the garage bench while Chris finished the polishing and then they all set off. Haffertee and Howl perched on the top of the back seat and looked out of the windows. The World Outside was full of all kinds of things.

The trees were waving their arms and the green grass seemed to stretch for ever. Then they began to pass telegraph poles and lamp posts and road signs. A great muddle and mix of things. Houses smiled at them as they passed. Hurrying people crowded the pavements. The shops were so full of exciting things

48

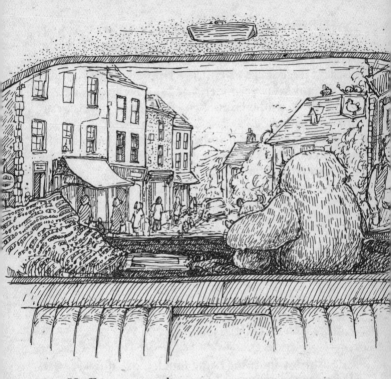

that Haffertee gasped.

'Is this really the World Outside?' he asked.

'Yes,' said Howl, slowly. 'And a very interesting place it is.'

Haffertee felt quite sure it was. There was so much to see and to watch and to touch.

'When are you going to College?' asked Haffertee, as the little car stopped outside the Post Office.

'There's a lot of packing to do first,' said Chris. 'But I hope to leave on Saturday morning.'

Haffertee began to think about Saturday morning. Chris Diamond and Saturday morning and the World Outside. He thought about them all the way back to the garage at Hillside House.

'Thank you very much,' he said to Chris as he and Howl Owl climbed out of the little car. 'It was great fun having a ride.'

Chris nodded and smiled and began to polish the other side of his little grey car. He was pleased he had shown Haffertee the village. Saturday morning was not very far away now, and he would be off to start a new life of his own.

Saturday morning came much more quickly than Haffertee thought possible. Suddenly everyone in the Diamond family was standing at the bottom of the garden steps to say 'Goodbye' to Chris. He seemed very happy as he put his boxes and cases into the little grey car. Then a final checking of this and that to the engine under the hood, and Chris was gone. The little car was buzzing along the road – round the corner and out of sight.

Chris Diamond was on his way to the World Outside.

The whole family turned back up the steps and into the house. Everyone seemed unusually quiet and thoughtful.

Haffertee went straight to Yo's room and settled himself quietly in his Very Own Box. He wanted a careful think about that World Outside.

He looked round at the pictures of his friends on the wall and on the table. He looked at Chris especially, and smiled back at him. Haffertee really was happy at Hillside House. But . . . the World Outside looked *very* exciting.

'*I'm* going to take a good look at that World Outside,' Haffertee said firmly to everyone in the pictures. 'I want to see it for myself. All those smiling houses and hurrying people. The tall poles and waving trees! The soft green grass and the shops bursting with things! Yes! Yes! *I'm* going to look at

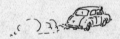

the World Outside. If Chris can do it, so can I.'

Haffertee Hamster Diamond had made up his mind.

# Spotted Dog
# to the Rescue

When Haffertee made up his mind to do something, he usually did it. Right now he had made up his mind to leave Hillside House! It wasn't that he didn't like it. He loved it. He hadn't quarrelled with anyone, and he certainly wasn't angry. But if Chris Diamond could go off by himself to see the World Outside, then so could Haffertee! He wanted to look at it face to face. He wanted to see it for himself.

Diamond Yo tried to make him change his mind. But she didn't succeed.

Howl Owl was very sad. 'It's dangerous,' he said. 'Remember the Bramble Wilderness. Remember Spotted Dog!' But Haffertee wouldn't listen. Mark and even Fran joined in trying to persuade him not to go. But Haffertee's mind was made up.

So they all stopped persuading and began advising and helping him instead. Rabbearmonklio got an old coat from a toy soldier friend to keep out the rain. Howl Owl drew him a map. Diamond Yo made a shoulder bag to carry his food in, and Pops cut him a sturdy walking-stick. Everyone gave him something for his journey.

Haffertee was very pleased with them all.

When the time came to leave, a great crowd of friends gathered at the hole in the wire fence to see him off.

Haffertee didn't look back. He strode down the path into the Bramble Wilderness with his stick and his coat and his very special bag slung over his shoulder.

Mrs Ellington Purrswell and her three kittens went a little way with him. Then they came back. Haffertee turned the corner past the stinging-nettle patch and was gone. Slowly everyone went back to

the house. It wouldn't be the same without Haffertee . . .

Several days went by. Howl Owl heard news from his many friends. Haffertee was well. He was on his way to the Pottinger Wood. Then, suddenly, the messages stopped! The days went by and still there was no news. No one had seen him. Diamond Yo began to get worried. Whatever could have happened?

There was worse to come. Howl Owl came back one afternoon with Haffertee's special bag – the one Yo had made. It was muddy and torn and the strap was broken. It was quite empty.

The very next day Islington Weasel came to the house with the walking-stick Pops had cut for Haffertee. It was half broken and there were traces of fur on it.

Then, last of all, Samson came in with Haffertee's new soldier-coat – it was covered in dirt and blackberry juice and there was Haffertee's fur on the collar.

*Whatever* could have happened? Had he been robbed? Whoever would do such a thing? Whatever it was, Haffertee had disappeared and his things had been taken from him.

The whole house was concerned.

The whole house was in an upset.

Mrs Ellington Purrswell hunted the Pottinger Wood. Samson wandered through the Bramble Wilderness. Everyone waited anxiously for news.

When no news came, Howl Owl had the best idea yet.

'Let's ask Spotted Dog to help us,' he said. 'He had a good sniff of Haffertee that time in the rhubarb patch. Surely he could follow Haffertee's trail.'

And that's just what happened. Spotted Dog was asked and Spotted Dog followed the trail. It led right through the woods and out on the other side. Down into a muddy ditch with just a little trickle of water at the bottom, then into an old hedgehog bed under a great overhanging tree-root.

It was there that Spotted Dog found Haffertee. Badly bruised and shaken, but alive. Haffertee couldn't believe his eyes when he saw Spotted Dog. He was so pleased to see someone from home, he wasn't at all afraid.

'Oh, Spotted Dog,' he said. 'I am glad you've come. I was caught by robbers in the Pottinger Wood and I've been too scared to move.'

Diamond Yo came running through the woods the moment she heard that Haffertee had been found. She was so very pleased. She lifted Haffertee gently, laid him in a nice soft duster, and very carefully

brought him home to Hillside House.

That night everyone joined in the welcome home song.

    'Haffertee's home again.
    Haffertee's home again.
    Thank you God, O thank you God!
    Haffertee's home again.'

And no one sang louder than Howl Owl and Diamond Yo.

# The Party
# in the Garage

The whole house was buzzing with excitement. There was going to be a party in the garage and everyone was invited. It was to celebrate Haffertee's coming home. Diamond Yo wanted everyone at Hillside House to be there.

All the toys from the Toy Cupboard had been invited.

The gerbils had been asked to come, and so had Rabbearmonklio.

Mrs Ellington Purrswell and the kittens were sure to be there.

Samson the tortoise . . . everyone.

Yo was going to make it a really wonderful time.

Everyone was busy with the preparations.

Ma Diamond had promised all sorts of good things to eat and Pops said he'd sing a few songs. Mark was tidying up and sweeping the floor.

It was going to be a wonderful party. Diamond Yo was quite sure about that. Haffertee would be the Very Special Person. Fran was giving him an extra-careful wash and brush.

The kittens had a powder bath to make their fur sparkle, and Rabbearmonklio brushed his tail!

Everyone was so pleased to have Haffertee back safe and sound from his adventure in the Pottinger Wood. They were all ready to enjoy themselves at the party.

But no one seemed to know where Howl Owl was.

He had been so pleased to see Haffertee home again that he had stayed awake all night just keeping an eye on Haffertee's Very Own Box. He was afraid that Haffertee might wander off again into the World Outside.

Now Howl was missing.

Diamond Yo took no notice at first. But when it came to two o'clock and there was still no sign of Howl, she began to wonder what had happened.

And then, at five-past two, Howl Owl appeared. He had a parcel under his wing. It was wrapped in sparkling paper and tied up with coloured ribbon.

'This is a present for Haffertee,' he explained. 'He mustn't open it until the party.'

Haffertee was so excited. He couldn't wait for the party to begin.

And when it did, he was in such a hurry to open his parcel that he tore the paper and got all twisted up in the ribbon. He was so anxious to know what his present was.

It was a picture – a picture of the World Outside.

'Ma drew it,' said Howl Owl. 'And I coloured it in. I took it to the loft so that you wouldn't see.

And I didn't finish it till two o'clock.'

Haffertee held it up and looked at it closely.

The trees were waving their arms and the green grass seemed to stretch for ever. There were telegraph poles and lamp posts and road signs. There were aeroplanes and boats and motor cars. Smiling houses, crowded pavements and shops full of exciting things.

And underneath the picture there was a poem. It had been written by Samson the tortoise. Haffertee read it out loud.

    'The World Outside is beautiful;
    A great place to explore.
    Surprises and excitement there.
    No one could ask for more.
    But sometimes it's a pleasure
    To forget the World Outside
    And come back to a happy home
    With all your friends inside.'

Haffertee swallowed hard. There seemed to be a lump of something in his throat. He looked round slowly at all his friends and smiled. He didn't say a word.

It was Diamond Yo who spoke.

'Thank you, God, that Haffertee's home again,' she said – then, firmly, to Haffertee: 'This is where you belong.'

And Haffertee knew she was right.

The
Diamond
Family

Fran          Ma

Diamond Yo
with
Hafferkee and
Howl Out

Pops          Mark          Chris.